I Want My Tooth

Tony Ross

More Little Princess books

I Want My Potty

Wash Your Hands!

I Don't Want to Go to Bed!

I Want My Pacifier

First American Edition 2005
by Kane/Miller Book Publishers Inc.
La Jolla, California

First published in 2002 by Andersen Press Ltd., Great Britain
Text and illustrations copyright © Tony Ross 2002

Library of Congress Control Number: 2005923366

Printed and Bound in Singapore by Tien Wah Press, Ltd.

1 2 3 4 5 6 7 8 9 10

ISBN 1-929132-85-9

I Want My Tooth

Tony Ross

Kane/Miller
BOOK PUBLISHERS

The Little Princess had WONDERFUL teeth.

She counted them every morning. Then she brushed them . . .

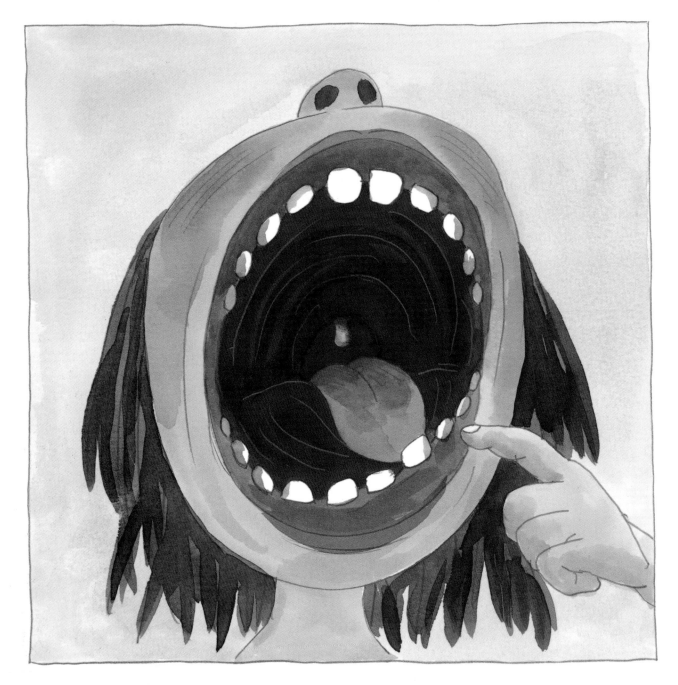

. . . then she counted them again. She had TWENTY.

Some of her friends had fewer than twenty teeth.
But THEY were not ROYAL.

Her little brother, who WAS royal, had NO teeth at all.

"Haven't I got wonderful teeth?" asked the Little Princess. "In smart straight lines," answered the General. "Shipshape and Bristol fashion," answered the Admiral.

"Haven't I got wonderful teeth?" asked the Little Princess.
"ROYAL teeth!" answered the King.

So every night, the Little Princess brushed the royal teeth again.

"You have wonderful teeth because you eat all the right things,"
said the Cook.

"You can count them if you like," said the Little Princess.
"One ... two ... three ... four ...

"HEY," said the Cook. "This one WOBBLES!"

"AAAAAGH!" screamed the Little Princess. "One WOBBLES!"

"AAAAAGH!" screamed the Maid. "One WOBBLES!"

The wobbly tooth wobbled MORE each day.

But the wobbly tooth didn't hurt,
and soon the Little Princess enjoyed wobbling it.

And she wobbled it and wobbled it,
until the terrible day the wobbly tooth disappeared.

"I WANT MY TOOTH!" cried the Little Princess.

"You can have mine," said the Dentist, "until your new one comes along!"
"I want my tooth NOW!" said the Little Princess.

Everybody in the Palace searched for the missing tooth . . .

. . . but it was NOWHERE to be found.
"I WANT MY TOOTH!" cried the Little Princess.

"SHE WANTS HER TOOTH!" cried the Maid.

"It's all right," said the Little Princess. "I've FOUND it . . .

. . . HE'S got it!"